In the storm drain . . .

"Let's go see what those eyes belong to," Mike said. "Are you guys coming?"

Just then the eyes disappeared.

"What happened?" the Big T said. "Where'd they go?"

We heard something in the dark, a sort of scritchy-scratchy sound at first and then a kind of clickety-clackety sound, like the noise hard claws make scraping over concrete.

"What's that sound?" the Big T said. "I don't like that noise."

I didn't like it much, either, but Mike Gonzo wasn't bothered in the least. "It's running from us, whatever it is," he said. "That's why we can't see its eyes."

"Oh, yeah?" the Big T said. "Then what are those?"

I looked ahead of us, so far ahead that whatever had been running couldn't possibly have gotten that far away.

I saw two more eyes, glowing as red as the first two.

BILL CRIDER

A MINSTREL®
BOOK

Published by POCKET BOOKS
New York   London   Toronto   Sydney   Tokyo   Singapore

A MINSTREL PAPERBACK *Original*

A Minstrel Book published by
POCKET BOOKS, a division of Simon & Schuster Inc.
1230 Avenue of the Americas, New York, NY 10020

ISBN: 0-671-53651-6

First Minstrel Books printing November 1996

10 9 8 7 6 5 4 3 2 1

Cover art by Broeck Steadman

Printed in the U.S.A.

*For Elizabeth, Robert, and Nancy Romig
and Susan and Clifton Lee*

Chapter 1

The Whole Truth and Nothing But

I know you've probably read in the newspapers about what happened here in Midgeville, and the reason I'm writing this is to set the record straight. The reporters got some of the details right, but they didn't get everything down exactly the way it was.

Of course, the kind of papers that gave the story the most space were the kind your mother tells you to stop reading when you're standing in line at the supermarket.

You know the ones I mean. They're the ones with headlines like RUSH LIMBAUGH MEETS WITH

UFO ALIENS or TODDLER LOSES BEAUTY CONTEST, BITES OFF WINNER'S EAR. They even have photos.

But we made the respectable papers, too, and even those had headlines that said SEWER MONSTER ATTACKS IN MIDGEVILLE.

Now, that's what I mean about the way they get things wrong. There wasn't any monster in the sewers at all.

It was in the storm drains.

And, if you want to be completely honest about it, there wasn't just one monster.

There were two.

Plus, they really didn't cause any trouble at all while they were actually *in* the storm drains. It's pretty hard for anything to bother anyone down there. Nothing really happened until they got *out* of the drains.

Anyway, it all started when Mike Gonzo—

Wait.

I said I was going to set things straight, so I'd better get the part about Mike's name right, too.

There's no one named Mike Gonzo in Midgeville. His name's really Mike Chilton. He's thirteen years old, just like me, and he's skinny like me, and he has his red hair that falls around his face. We just call him Mike Gonzo because of the way he acts.

He'll do anything. That's right. *Anything,* though I think that some of the stories about him are probably exaggerated. I mean, I'm not sure exactly how those twelve goats got out into the middle of the baseball diamond during that game last spring, and it was too bad about the one that butted Coach Emerson, but no one ever proved that Mike had anything to do with it.

But he certainly is one totally fearless guy, I have to admit that much.

Whenever you see or hear one of those warnings that say, "Kids, don't try this at home," you can bet that Mike will be trying it at home or somewhere else—which is why we were down in the storm drains in the first place.

You probably noticed that "we" in the last sentence and guessed that Mike wasn't down in the storm drains all by himself.

Well, you're right. A friend of ours we call the Big T is usually with him. I am, too.

I don't know about the Big T, but I'm usually

with Mike when he does a lot of things because I have a "character weakness." That's what my father calls it: a character weakness.

"I just don't know about you, Robert," my dad says. He always calls me Robert, even if everyone else just calls me Bob. "You seem very easily led by other young men. I suppose it's a character weakness."

He's probably right.

And he's right about me being easily led, too. Mike Gonzo can talk me into just about anything, but then I don't feel too bad about that because he can talk nearly *anybody* into just about anything.

When he talks about doing things, his eyes get really big behind his glasses, and that red hair of his seems to become just a little redder, and there's something about his voice that changes and makes you believe every single word he says.

I remember the summer after sixth grade, when Mike wanted some peaches. He suggested that we borrow some from Mr. Albany, who had a peach tree in his backyard.

Now, I always had the idea that "borrowing"

4

had something to do with "paying back," and the way Mike explained it to me was that we would pay Mr. Albany back as soon as we got some more peaches to pay him back with.

Somehow it didn't sound quite right to me, but the more Mike talked, the bigger his eyes got, and he started to wave his hands around, and his voice got . . . I don't know, bigger somehow, and you could practically hear a band way off somewhere in the distance playing "The Stars and Stripes Forever."

So we borrowed the peaches.

Believe me, it wasn't easy to get them down from the tree without being seen, and as I remember it, I was the one who did most of the work. The peaches tasted really good, though, and I thought everything was cool until my mother told me that Mr. Albany had called her about it. He didn't mention borrowing at all. Instead he used the word *stealing*, and I had to mow his yard three times to earn the money to pay for those peaches.

My father said he was disappointed in me for letting myself be so easily led, and to tell the truth, I was sort of disappointed in myself. But the way Mike had made things sound, we weren't really doing anything wrong.

The Big T may not have a character weakness, but he's no better than I am when it comes to letting Mike talk him into things, even though he's a lot bigger than me. He's a lot bigger than Mike, too. For that matter, he's a lot bigger than nearly anyone else we know, and he plays in the defensive line for the Midgeville Middle School Musk Oxen football team. He's an end.

He's only thirteen, just like me and Mike, but he's about a foot taller than we are, and he weighs about one hundred and eighty pounds, only some of which is fat. His real name is Geoffrey Thomas, but how many kids do you know with a name like Geoffrey? He's big, and his last name starts with a "T," so that's how he got the nickname.

His only real weakness as a football player is that he's very nearsighted, and he thinks glasses make defensive linemen look like sissies, so he won't wear them during a game. So sometimes when he charges into the offensive backfield, he accidentally tackles one of the officials instead of the guy with the ball.

He's going to get contacts one of these days, and we all think that then he'll be a real star. For now, it's getting harder and harder to find a group of officials that will work at one of our games.

Anyway, you'd think a guy that big and strong, and a football player besides, wouldn't be so easy to talk into doing weird things. But the Big T was right down there in the storm drains with me and Mike Gonzo.

You have to understand, though, that while Mike might do some dumb things, he would never do anything *really* stupid.

He'd never climb into the storm drains when it was raining, for example, and there was a river of water down there. He knows better than that. And he wouldn't try to talk me into going with him in a case like that because, well, I'd just laugh at him, character weakness or not.

So would the Big T.

I seem to be getting a little off the subject of the sewer monster here, but I think you need to know all this other stuff before we get to that part. So let me tell you what we were doing in the storm drains in the first place.

Where we live, there's a lot of rain, and there's a long ditch in front of the houses. Where the ditch ends, a big concrete pipe makes a dark circle that leads under the street.

If you crawl into the pipe—which is pretty hard to resist if someone for the city work crew has taken off the grate to clean it and forgotten to put it back on—you can smell the darkness. It has a damp, musty smell, like water and mud and wet leaves all mixed together, and if you yell, you can hear your voice echo up and down the drain.

The bottom of the drain is about a three-foot drop from the end of the pipe, and if you toss a rock into the drain, you can hear it clatter off the concrete side before it plops into the soft mud or splashes into the thin trickle of water at the bottom.

It's dark in the drain, so the mud never really dries, and it's a lot cooler down there than it is outside, especially on a sunny day in the summer, like the day I want to tell you about, when Mike Gonzo was dropping rocks into the drain and waiting for his eyes to get used to the darkness.

Sometimes, if you wait awhile, you can see the bottom of the drain. And sometimes you can even see things in there.

Once we saw a frog. It was a pretty big frog, green and sort of shiny, with big pop eyes and those funny froggy legs with knees that are higher than its body.

We almost went after it, but when we tossed a rock in its direction it hopped away, plopping into the mud, and we knew we could never catch it.

But on the day I'm talking about, we didn't see a frog. We saw a wallet.

That wallet was why we went into the drain in the first place. If it hadn't been for that, we'd never have found the monsters, and Midgeville would've probably been a much quieter place to live.

But the wallet was there, and it was going to stay there for a while. It wasn't going to hop away like the frog.

However, it was likely that the next big rain

would wash it down to the river, or to wherever the drain emptied. Then it would be gone forever.

Naturally, Mike couldn't let that happen. He just had to get it. It hadn't rained in a while so it was relatively dry down there.

And, of course, he talked me and the Big T into going with him.

Chapter 2

Grape Juice

I can't see anything," the Big T said.

"That's because you're out there, and we're in here," Mike said. His voice echoed down the storm drain.

"Well, let me in there, then," the Big T said. "I want to see it."

"Come on," Mike said to me. "You first."

Mike and I backed out of the pipe, sort of shimmying along on our stomachs. There was room for two people our size in the pipe, or for one person the size of the Big T.

When we got back up, the Big T said, "You sure it's a wallet you saw? It's awful dark in there." He was sweating pretty good, and there were dark stains on the front of his Metallica T-shirt.

"I know a wallet when I see one," Mike said, blinking his eyes a little because of the bright sun. "And that's what it is, all right. Isn't it, Bob?"

"Sure it is," I said. "A brown one, with some kind of picture on it."

"I never saw a wallet like that," the Big T said.

"No, and you never will," Mike said. "Not unless you take a look down there."

The Big T got down on his hands and knees and crawled up to the circle. Then he lay down and slithered in. It was kind of funny to watch him, since he wasn't exactly built for slithering. Slithering was more for wiry types like me and Mike.

After he entered the circle, the Big T lay still for a few seconds. Then he called out, "I still can't see any wallet."

His voice sounded really strange, all deep and hollow because of the echo from the concrete walls.

"No wonder you can't see anything," Mike said. "You're so nearsighted, you couldn't see it if it was sitting on your nose."

The Big T made a kind of grunting noise and started slithering backward, like he was coming back up. He was touchy about his eyesight and those glasses he had to wear.

He wanted to think of himself as a really cool, good-looking dude, but what he really sort of looked like was a bulldog with a bad squint. He blamed the squint on the glasses.

"I was just kidding," Mike said before the Big T could get out. "You can't see anything because it's so dark in there. What we need is a flashlight."

He was looking at me when he said the part about the flashlight because we were less than a block away from my house.

"If we had a flashlight," he went on, "we could see the wallet really well. We might even be able to go down there and get it."

"I'm not so sure that's a good idea," the Big T said as he hoisted himself up out of the pipe. "I mean, you never know what you might meet up with down there. Remember that frog?"

"You aren't going to tell me you're afraid of a frog, are you?" Mike said. He had that determined look in his eyes that I'd seen before. I knew he'd go after that wallet, no matter what. "What do you think, that he'll *hop* on you or something?"

"I'm not afraid of a frog," the Big T said. "But they give you warts, don't they? Warts don't look so great, and they might even itch." He looked down at his hands as if he were wondering what they would look like with warts on them. "I don't think I'd like having warts," he mumbled.

Mike laughed. "Frogs don't give you warts, Big T. Warts are caused by a virus."

"Oh," the Big T said. "Are you sure about that?"

"Of course I'm sure," Mike said, but that didn't really mean anything. He was always sure, even when he was dead wrong. He looked at me. "Now what about that flashlight?"

"All right," I said. "I'll get one. You guys want to come with me? We can get something to drink."

That sounded like a good idea to both of

them, especially the Big T, the front of whose T-shirt was now stained with dirt and grass as well as sweat. Metallica wasn't looking so good, but then they don't look very good even when they're cleaned up.

When we got to my house, we went in through the garage door that leads to the back part of the house. My mother was there in the little room she calls the office.

It's really the fourth bedroom, but there aren't any beds in it. There's a desk with a computer and a printer and a modem, and there's another desk with a Rolodex and lots of pens and pencils and paper clips and stuff like that scattered around. My mother keeps the books for three or four businesses in town, but thanks to the computer and modem, she can do most of her work right there at home.

"What are you boys up to?" she said, looking up from the computer when we came in.

She didn't mean anything by saying that. It's what she always says. But the Big T is the kind of guy who takes any question literally and who always looks guilty. It's just a talent he has.

"Who, us?" he said, looking up at the ceiling and down at the floor and anywhere but at my mother. "We're not up to anything. Not a thing. Not us. And you can bet we're not thinking about getting a flashlight and going down the storm drain."

My mother swiveled her chair around and looked hard at the Big T for a second. And then her eyes landed on me. She has short black hair and black eyes that snap at you when she's upset.

"Robert Randall Ross!" she said. The eyes were snapping, all right. They usually are when she calls me by my full name. "You aren't planning to go down in that storm drain, I hope!"

"Well, uh, not exactly," I said. "I just thought, uh, I mean *we* just thought we might try to get something out of there. We might not have to actually go—"

"What he means is that there's a wallet in the storm drain," Mike said, interrupting me.

I didn't mind a bit. I was glad Mike jumped in to tell the truth.

"It could be that someone lost the wallet we

saw," he went on. "Or it could be that it was stolen. We just want to try to get it and return it to its rightful owner. It might have some important papers in it, or maybe even money and credit cards. The owner will be worried about it, I'm sure."

His voice was doing that trick it has, and his eyes were shining.

"Oh," my mother said. "Couldn't you just reach down and get it with a stick or something?"

"We'll certainly try," Mike said. "We wouldn't do anything foolish like going down in the storm drain unless all else failed."

He looked very sincere when he said it. I wished that I could talk to adults like that, but somehow they never seem to take me seriously the way they do Mike.

"Well, I suppose that if there is a wallet, and if it does belong to someone, then you should try to get it," my mother said.

"You're right," Mike said. "It's the only thing to do. And if there's any identification inside, we'll see that it gets back to the person who lost it."

17

"Just don't do anything foolish," my mother said.

"No way," Mike said. "We'll be very cautious."

"I'm sure you will," my mother said, turning back to the computer. "Why don't you have something to drink first?"

Mike nudged me with his elbow.

"Sure," I said. "Just what I was thinking. Let's go, guys."

We went. It had been a close call, but Mike Gonzo was never at a loss for words.

There was a bottle of grape juice in the refrigerator, so I got glasses for everyone and poured the juice.

The Big T took a drink and smiled with satisfaction. He had a little purple mustache above his upper lip.

I didn't mention it to him, though. I just went to get the flashlight, a rechargeable model that was plugged into a wall socket under the cabinet by the stove.

"What are you going to do with that?" my sister said.

I don't know where she came from. Sometimes I think she's some kind of witch who can just sort of appear out of nowhere.

Mike and the Big T both put their glasses down on the table and groaned when they heard her.

I didn't blame them one bit.

Chapter 3

My Sister

It's not that there's anything really wrong with my sister.

Here name's Laurie. She's two years younger than I am, but she looks a lot like me. She's skinny, and she has black eyes and black hair that kind of falls down in her face sometimes.

The only thing I can't stand about her, aside from that bad habit of popping up out of nowhere, is that she always thinks she knows everything. And she's very nosy.

"You still haven't told me what you're going to do with the flashlight," she said.

I realized that I was just standing there looking at the flashlight as if I were wondering how it got in my hand.

"Nothing," I said.

"You are, too. Nobody gets a flashlight for no reason." She looked over at the Big T. She knew just who to ask if she wanted a confession. "Geoffrey, what are you going to do?"

"Nothing," the Big T said, a little surprised to hear his real name. "We're just drinking grape juice, that's all. We aren't doing anything else, and we sure aren't going down in the—"

"What he means to say," Mike said, interrupting again, "is that while we have plans to do something, you are not included in those plans." He drank the last of his juice and put the glass down with a clunk. "Ready, guys?"

"Ready," the Big T and I said.

We started out of the kitchen.

"You'd better not leave without telling me what you're going to do," Laurie said.

We didn't say anything. We just kept on walking.

"Mom!" Laurie said.

She didn't say it very loud, hardly above a

whisper, but she said it loud enough to stop us. We turned to look at her.

"She's your sister," Mike said. His voice was very quiet, too. "So it's up to you. But I say we kill her."

He was only kidding.

I mean, I *think* he was only kidding. With Mike, you could never be absolutely sure about something like that.

Laurie didn't think he was. Her black eyes snapped just like my mother's, and she said, "Just you try it, Michael Chilton. I dee-double-dog-dare you." She stood there with her hands on her hips and her hair falling down across her face and stared at Mike.

He stared back for a while and then said, "All right. We won't kill her. But she can't go with us."

"Can, too," Laurie said. "If you try to stop me, I'll tell Mom you're being mean to me."

Mike looked at me and shook his head sorrowfully, as if it were somehow my fault that I had a sister.

"All right," he said. "You can go."

"Good. Now where are we going?" Laurie asked.

"Not so fast," Mike said. "First you have to agree to follow the rules."

"What rules?" Laurie said.

"Our rules."

Laurie thought about it. "How many rules are there?" she said.

"Just two."

"What are they?"

"Number one, keep out of our way. Number two, keep your mouth shut."

"I'll keep out of the way," Laurie said.

"And keep your mouth shut," Mike said. "You forgot about that one."

Laurie shook her head. "I didn't forget anything. I'll keep out of the way, but I won't keep my mouth shut."

Mike was getting that stubborn look again, but the Big T said, "Aw, let her come with us, Mike. If she keeps out of the way, she won't bother us."

Mike shrugged. "If that's the way you want it," he said. "But I think we're making a big mistake."

I thought we were, too, but I didn't say anything. I happened to know that it wouldn't do any good. I'd been around my sister long enough to know that if anyone was a match for Mike Gonzo, it was Laurie Ross.

"So where are we going?" Laurie said.

"Does it make any difference?" Mike said.

"Not really, but I want to know."

"We're going down in the storm drain," I said.

"The storm drain? What for? It's muddy and dark in there. You might get some kind of weird disease."

"We saw a frog in there once," the Big T said. "I heard that frogs cause warts. You'd look pretty bad with warts all over you."

"You can't scare me by saying that, Geoffrey," Laurie said. "Warts are caused by a virus, not by frogs."

"I've heard that," the Big T said. "But you never can tell."

"Are we going to talk about frogs, or are we getting out of here?" Mike said.

"Getting out of here," I said, leading the way.

"Be careful," Mom called when we walked by her office.

"We will," I said.

Laurie didn't say anything. I don't think she wanted Mom to know she was with us, because Mom has a sort of double standard about some things. While she really might not mind if I went into the storm drain to look for a wallet, she wouldn't want Laurie down there. It was the kind of thing Mom thought was all right for a boy, but not for a girl.

I didn't see the difference, myself.

When we got to the circular opening, Laurie looked at it skeptically.

"We're going in there?" she said.

"Some of us are," Mike told her. "You can go home now if you're afraid."

"Ha ha," she said. "You wish." She kept on looking at the opening. "I'm just wondering about one thing."

"What?" I said.

"What if someone gets stuck in there?"

The Big T's face got red.

"Remember," Mike said, "I wanted to kill her."

"Ha ha again," Laurie said.

"Anyway," I said, "no one will get stuck. We've been down the drains before."

"Okay. I believe you. Who goes first?"

"I do," Mike said, and he bent down and slithered feet first into the pipe.

Chapter 4

Eyes in the Dark

It was very cool down in the storm drain, a kind of damp coolness like you might feel in a cave, but that was the only cavelike thing about it. There were no stalagmites standing on the floor or stalactites hanging from the ceiling. The walls were smooth concrete, and there was mud on the bottom. There was a kind of damp smell, too, like some rooms in old houses get after a heavy rain.

My feet squished in the mud, and I moved out of the way, because here came the Big T right behind me. His feet made a loud splatting sound when he landed. I felt a glob of mud slap against the leg of my jeans.

I looked around. There was light coming in from the entrance, and Mike had the flashlight on, so I could see a little. Our shadows bounced around the dark walls.

It was strange being down there under the ground. We were practically under the street, and we could hear the swishing sound the cars made as they drove above our heads.

Mike was shining the flashlight all over as he looked around the drain, which was a lot like a round tunnel.

"Can you see the wallet?" Laurie asked. Her head was hanging over the edge of the entrance pipe, and her voice sounded deep and hollow.

"Why don't you come down and look for yourself?" Mike answered.

"I've changed my mind," Laurie said. "That mud is nasty, and I don't want to get it on my shoes."

Well, I was just as glad she wasn't coming, to tell the truth. And I didn't blame her for not wanting to get muddy. The stuff was deeper than I'd thought it would be, and I was afraid it might seep in over the tops of my sneakers.

"There it is," Mike said. He held the light

steady on the wallet, about five feet away, and nodded to the Big T.

First the Big T just stared at the wallet and didn't budge. Then he realized we were all waiting, and he sort of tiptoed through the mud over to it. He picked it up and held it out at arm's length. "Gross," he said, handing the wallet to me.

It was gross, all right. It was wet and smelly, and it was sort of like holding something that's been under the water a long time, rotting away. When I opened it, it practically came apart in my hands.

"There's no telling how long that thing's been down here," Mike said. "Is there any identification in it?"

I looked at the little plastic pockets where you put pictures and things. They were all cracked and empty.

"No," I said.

"Too bad. How about money?" Mike asked.

I looked into the bill compartment, but there was nothing there except a thin coating of slime.

"No money, either," I said.

"Rats," the Big T said. "Look in the secret compartment."

"There's no secret compartment," I said.

"What kind of wallet is it if it doesn't have a secret compartment?" the Big T said. "Where can you hide stuff?"

"Maybe whoever owned it didn't have anything to hide," Mike said. "Give it to your sister, Bob. Maybe she can find out who owned it."

"I don't want that dirty thing," Laurie said, but she was too late. I'd already tossed the wallet up to her.

She ducked out of the way, and the wallet landed with a wet splat just about where her head had been.

"You were trying to hit me," she said.

"No, I wasn't," I said.

"Right," the Big T said. "It was just a lucky shot."

"Well, I'm not touching it," Laurie said. "And you'd better come out of there right now."

I didn't normally agree with my sister about things like that, but I was all for getting out.

The mud was slopping around my feet, and I could see a little trickle of water running through the gunk in the middle of the storm drain. No wonder it was so sloppy.

"I guess she's right," I said. "We'd better get out."

Of course even before I said it, I knew that we wouldn't really go back outside. Not yet. Not with Mike Gonzo around.

"Wait a minute," he said. "What's the big rush? Haven't we always wanted to see what's down here?"

Nobody answered him.

"Well, haven't we?"

"I, uh, I guess so," the Big T said, probably thinking about frogs.

"Well, we're down here now," Mike pointed out, "and we might not ever have a reason to come back. Let's take a look around."

Before we could say anything, he was shining the light around the tunnel. It bounced off the damp walls and was reflected back at us off the thin stream of water at our feet.

Then Mike pointed it farther down the tunnel, and that's when we saw them—two round circles, very red, gleaming at us out of the darkness.

"Whoa!" said the Big T. "What's that?"

"Eyes," Mike said.

Do you know how an animal's eyes look in the dark when a light hits them, sort of round and red and shiny? That's what we were looking at.

They were eyes, all right.

Chapter 5

Claws

The Big T was backing up fast. So was I. Not Mike Gonzo, though.

"Let's go see what those eyes belong to," he said.

"You'd better not," Laurie said from just overhead. "You're going to get in trouble."

"Boy, I'm glad I don't have a sister," Mike said, shaking his head. He started toward the eyes. "Are you guys coming?"

We were. I don't know why, but we were. We started forward again, following right behind him, our feet slipping and sliding on the

33

slimy mud that clung to the sloping concrete sides of the drain.

Away off in the distance, about three blocks, there was a small round circle of light. That was where the underground drain opened into an uncovered drain that ran alongside the street for five or six blocks. After a big rain, when most of the water had run out, the open drain was a pretty good place to catch tadpoles, so we'd been there before.

The two glistening eyes were between us and the opening, but at least I knew there was a way out besides the way we came in. I wasn't really very worried about the eyes. I thought they probably belonged to a frog, which just goes to show how wrong you can be sometimes.

"You'd better come back here, Robert Randall Ross," Laurie called, her voice echoing down the pipe after me.

That was another one of her irritating habits, calling me by my full name like that. She just does it because our mother does and because she knows it aggravates me.

I didn't even answer her. We were getting

closer to the eyes, and I wanted to see what they were. I was still thinking about a frog, or maybe a poor kitten that had gotten lost and wandered into the drain. We could rescue it and take it home.

Just then, the eyes disappeared.

"What happened?" the Big T said. "Where'd they go?"

We heard something in the dark, a sort of scritchy-scratchy sound at first and then a kind of clickety-clackety sound, like the noise sharp claws might make if they were scraping over concrete.

"What's that sound?" the Big T said. "I don't like that noise."

I didn't like it much, either, but Mike Gonzo wasn't bothered in the least.

"It's running from us, whatever it is," he said. "It's turned its back on us. That's why we can't see its eyes."

"Oh, yeah?" the Big T said. "Then what are those?"

I looked ahead of us and saw two more eyes, glowing just as red as the first two. But they were too far away to be the same eyes as the first set we had seen.

"Whatever it is," Mike said, realizing the same thing, "there must be two of them."

"Oh, great," the Big T said. "That's really great." He didn't sound scared, exactly, but then he didn't sound too happy about things, either.

I wasn't all that happy, myself. I was pretty sure frogs didn't have claws. And frogs didn't run away. They hopped.

But it could be a cat, I told myself. A poor helpless little kitten. I told myself that, but I didn't really believe it.

"Maybe we'd better just turn around and go on back," I said.

"What?" Mike said. "And not find out what those things are? You must be kidding."

The Big T put out a hand and grabbed Mike's arm. The flashlight beam wavered all around the tunnel, and then Mike stopped.

"He's not kidding," the Big T said. "It's his flashlight, after all. If he wants to go back, then we should go back."

The darkness had closed in all around us

now. The light coming in from the place where we had entered was behind us, and the opening to the outside was still more than a block away. The flashlight beam seemed to be getting dimmer, somehow.

It was a spooky feeling to be there under the ground, to hear the cars swish past on the street above us, to think about whatever it was that had red eyes and claws that scrabbled across the concrete.

Mike shined the flashlight in the Big T's face. It hit his glasses and turned them silvery gold. It looked as if there were no eyes behind the lenses.

That was a little scary, even for Mike. He lowered the light.

"We aren't that far from the end of the tunnel," Mike said. "We might as well go on. Anyway, whatever that thing is, it's just as scared of us as we are of it."

"I wouldn't bet on that," I said. I was still thinking about the sound those claws had made.

"Hey, there's nothing to worry about," Mike

37

stated matter-of-factly. "Did you see how close to the ground those eyes are? How could anything that small hurt us?"

He turned around and pointed the light down the tunnel. It reflected off four red eyes that seemed to be watching our every move.

Chapter 6

The Things in the Drain

Alligators!" the Big T said. "It's alligators!"

That's what they were, all right. Two alligators, crouching there in the mud at the bottom of the storm drain, staring at us with fiery red eyes.

The fact that they were there isn't as strange as you might think, really. Where we live, there are alligators all around. They're in the rivers and the bayous and the lakes, and more than once they've stopped rush hour traffic by lying in the middle of the road and refusing to budge. Hardly anyone wants to tangle with an alligator, even in a car. In a standoff the car usually loses.

Of course, the two we were looking at weren't really very *big* alligators. They looked plenty big to us, but they weren't the kind to tie up traffic for any length of time. One of them was probably not even three feet long. The other might have been a little bigger, maybe half a foot longer.

But don't get the wrong idea. Even an alligator of that size can do plenty of damage if it wants to. If one of them were to clamp its jaws around your foot, there wouldn't be any way you could persuade it to let go until it felt like it, and it might not feel like it for a long time. And when it did let go, well, you wouldn't be doing any running for quite a while. You probably wouldn't even be doing any *walking*.

Even Mike, who usually didn't hesitate, must have been thinking of what alligators could do, because he came to a complete stop as soon as he saw what was looking at us.

"We'd better get out of here," the Big T said. He turned around to leave. Facing an offensive line on the football field was one thing, but facing alligators in a dark storm drain was something else again.

I knew exactly how he felt. "He's right," I said. "Come on, Mike. It's time to go back where we came from."

Naturally, Mike didn't budge. He stood there, thinking things over. "Wait a minute," he said.

"Wait for what?" the Big T asked. "If we stand around here any longer, they'll attack. I saw this special about alligators on the Discovery Channel. They'll attack you and drag you under. Then they'll stuff you in an underwater cave or an old log until you rot. When they think you're all gooshy and decomposed, they'll come back and eat you."

He stopped and looked at both of us, though I don't think he could see us very well in the dark. "It happens all the time," he said.

"Drag you under what?" Mike said, pointing the flashlight at our feet. "I don't think there's room under this mud for you."

"You can joke about my size all you want to," the Big T said. "I'm getting out of here."

"Besides," Mike said, "I saw that same special. It was about crocodiles, not alligators."

"What's the difference?" the Big T said.

"Well, I don't remember exactly. But there is a difference. Something about the teeth."

I wish he hadn't mentioned the teeth. All during their argument, the two alligators had just been sitting there watching us, not moving at all, but when Mike mentioned teeth, the bigger one opened its mouth.

The flashlight beam sparkled off its teeth, which were very white and very pointed.

"That does it," the Big T said. "I'm gone, like a cool breeze."

He started back down the tunnel.

"You can leave if you want to," Mike said. "But think about this. If we just leave, there'll be two alligators on the loose in Midgeville. And we'll be responsible."

The Big T stopped. "It's not our fault they're here," he said over his shoulder. "We didn't have anything to do with it."

"But we know they're here," Mike said. "It might not be our fault, but we should do something about them."

"We can call the Animal Control officer," the Big T said. "It's her job to take care of stuff like this. She'll know what to do."

Mike laughed. "Sure she will. But think about it. Is she going to believe a couple of kids if they call up and say there are alligators in the sewer?"

He had a point there, I thought. There were kids who liked to call up the Animal Control officer just to bother her. They were always reporting things like possums running loose in the school's cafeteria or raccoons ransacking the school's Dumpster. Kids got a big kick out of it when the officer showed up and the principal told her that there were no animal pests around, only human ones.

The Big T didn't care about any of that. "This isn't a sewer," he said.

"Okay, it's a storm drain," Mike said. "That's practically the same thing. She'd never believe us anyway."

"She'd have to check it out, though," the Big T insisted. "Even if she thought it was just a joke, she'd have to make sure."

"Maybe," Mike said. "Maybe not."

"So what do *you* think we should do, Mike?" I said. I was getting a little tired of listening to them argue, and all the while those alligator eyes were staring right at us, not moving, not blinking. "Do you want us to catch them ourselves?"

Mike started forward. "Let's see if they'll go outside. If they're right there in the open drain, then the Animal Control officer will have to believe us."

He took two steps, splatting his feet down hard in the mud.

The alligators turned and started skittering along the drain, their claws making that scrabbling sound as they went. They weren't moving very fast, though I'd heard that they could run faster than a horse over a short distance. I found out later how true that was.

"See?" Mike said. "They're afraid of us. We can make them go outside. Come on."

"You coming?" I asked the Big T.

"Well, I guess he's right," the Big T said. "Maybe we ought to do something. But I don't like it."

"I don't, either, but it might work," I said.

So there we all three went, slapping our feet down in the muck, sending it flying up on the walls and up on our clothes, and chasing the alligators slowly toward the light at the end of the tunnel.

They went right along, and it looked as if we were going to get away with it and maybe even be heroes.

I could see the headlines already: LOCAL YOUTHS SAVE MIDGEVILLE FROM ALLIGATOR INVASION! They'd probably have our pictures and everything, right there on the front page, and our families would be proud. Even Laurie.

Of course things didn't turn out exactly that way, and the headlines were a little bit different, as I mentioned earlier.

One reason was that there was someone out there in the open drain.

Several someones to be exact.

We didn't hear them until we were almost up to the opening, but we should have thought about it before. They were there all the time when the drain was dry, and it was dry now. I think I've already said that it hadn't rained for quite a while.

"They" were a bunch of local skateboarders. Everybody calls them skate rats. They even call themselves that.

There aren't very many good places to ride the boards in Midgeville. In fact, about the only places were the high school parking lot and the lot at the football stadium.

And of course the open storm drain.

The attraction of the drain wasn't the smooth bottom, not at all, even though you could ride down it for several blocks if you picked up all the trash that the water brought in.

No, the attraction was the steep sides. They had to contain a lot of water, so they must have been at least ten or maybe even twelve feet high. It was a lot different from riding on a level parking lot, where the only hazards were the occasional speed bumps.

The skate rats liked to perch at the top of one side of the drain and then careen down, scoot across the narrow bottom, and zoom up the opposite side.

If they survived that far, there were all sorts of tricks they could try.

Sometimes they would twist around in midair, the board somehow moving under their feet, and flash back down the side they'd just come up, then jet across the bottom and streak back up the side they'd come down at first.

Sometimes they'd soar up into the air, reach down, grab the board, and hold it over their heads as they landed flat on their feet.

I had to admit that it was fun to watch them, but I could never do anything like that myself. I'm a little clumsy and uncoordinated, and I can't even rub my stomach and pat my head at the same time. If I were to get on a skateboard, I'd be in the emergency room within five minutes and in traction not long after that.

Mike has done it, however. Naturally. I've seen him.

He even has an outfit like most of the skate rats wear. They all wear knee pads and elbow pads and hard plastic helmets that shine in the sun. I think I like the helmets best of all. They're red and yellow and green, and some of them have stripes on them of different colors. I'd like to ride a skateboard just to be able to wear a helmet like that.

Anyway, that was the noise we heard as we got near the end of the tunnel—the sound of the plastic skates as the boards swooshed down one side of the drain and up the other.

"We'd better stop," the Big T said. "We can't chase the alligators out there with people around."

He was right, and even Mike knew it.

So we stopped.

But it was too late. Alligators aren't exactly the most intelligent creatures in the world, even if they have been around since the time of the dinosaurs. Once they get going in one direction, it's not easy to change their tiny little minds.

In fact, they started to move a little faster after we stopped chasing them. We might as well have kept right on stomping in the mud.

"Come back here!" the Big T said, but it didn't do a bit of good.

We stood there watching as the alligators waddled right out of the tunnel and into the bright sun.

Chapter 7

Alligators on the Loose

We followed the alligators out of the tunnel, and I can honestly say I'd never seen anything quite like what happened next.

There were seven skateboarders there.

Five of them were standing at the top of the drain. Some of them were holding their boards, and the other boards were on the ground. The boards were all different colors, fluorescent yellow and red and green, and some of them were decorated with things like painted lightning bolts and flames and other things I couldn't quite make out. The T-shirts the skate rats were wearing were as colorful as the boards.

49

The shirts had slogans on them like THRASHER and DIE, YUPPIE SCUM.

The five skate rats who were standing at the top of the wall didn't see the alligators coming out of the tunnel because they were yelling encouraging words like "Cowabunga!" and "Banzai, Dudes!" and "Bodacious!" to the other two skateboarders, who were about six feet apart, crouched on their boards, and soaring down the concrete sides of the drain as fast as they could go.

Those two saw the alligators, all right, just before they got to the bottom, but it was much too late then to try to stop.

I don't know what the skate rats thought, but the alligators obviously weren't pleased with the sight of the speeding humans bearing down on them. The leathery reptiles stopped dead in their tracks, opened their mouths, and started hissing.

At least it sounded like hissing to me. It was an awfully scary sound, with all those teeth shining in the sun like they were.

The alligators were almost pretty out in the light, though, if you didn't look at the teeth.

Their bumpy skin was a sort of dark green on top and white on the bottom. Their eyes weren't red at all.

The skateboarders probably weren't thinking about the various aspects of alligator loveliness. To tell the truth, they looked more surprised than anything else. I could almost see their eyes widening.

I mean, imagine how *you'd* feel if you were speeding down a hill straight toward two alligators that had suddenly appeared out of nowhere who were hissing at you through their wide open mouths.

I have to give the skate rats credit for their skills and for remaining calm in the face of really weird circumstances.

I wouldn't have thought it was possible, but somehow they both seemed to levitate when they got to the bottom of the ditch. Their knees rose up almost to their chins. At the same time they reached down with their hands and grabbed their boards and lifted them right up, pressing them to the bottoms of their feet.

They went sailing over the alligators just as if they'd planned it that way, and the alligators raised their snouts and snapped at them, clicking their teeth together.

The riders lowered the boards and their feet just before they hit the concrete wall on the other side. It was really something to see, and it would have been even more spectacular if they had managed to skate on up to the top.

But it just didn't work out that way. I guess the angle must have been wrong or something.

As it was, instead of smoothly swooping up to the top of the drain, the two skate rats took a tumble, and all I could see were arms and legs and plastic protector pads whirling around and skateboards flying through the air.

Both boards landed safely away from the skaters and rolled back down the side of the drain, and one of the riders came to a stop about halfway up.

Unfortunately, the other rider started to tumble back down, right toward the alligators, who still had their mouths open. They looked almost cheerful, as if they were smiling while they waited.

For just a minute it seemed as if no one was going to do anything. The five skate rats at the top of the drain just stood there, watching. Their mouths were open, too, but not for the same reason as the alligators', and they weren't smiling.

And then Mike Gonzo took over.

"Let's go!" he said. "Come on, we've got to stop those alligators!"

I knew he was right. Someone had to do something, and it looked as if it had to be us. The trouble was that I didn't know how we were supposed to do anything, and I sure didn't have any idea of *what* to do.

As usual, however, that didn't matter. When Mike Gonzo said "go," I went.

Mike took off, and I followed, with the Big T right behind.

"You two help the one who fell," Mike said. "I'll take care of the alligators."

That sounded fine to me. I didn't want to associate with the alligators any more than was absolutely necessary.

I stepped up on the slanting side of the drain and ran toward the fallen skateboard rider, getting between him and the alligators. The Big T was beside me, and all we really had to do was stand there and let the rider roll into our legs, where he came to a stop.

While we were helping him up, Mike was poking at the alligators with one of the skateboards.

The alligators didn't seem very interested any longer. They made a halfhearted snap or two at the boards, and then they just waddled off down the drain.

The Big T and I each took a hand and pulled the skateboarder to his feet, and when he took his helmet off, we saw that he was a girl.

I know that sounds funny, but all along I'd been thinking that anybody who rode a skateboard would most likely be a boy, since it's a kind of rough sport, so I was naturally expecting to see a boy when he got up.

Instead I saw Brenda Tolson, a girl who was in our grade at school.

Ms. Austermont, our English teacher, has told us that thinking in stereotypes is lazy thinking and can get you in trouble. Maybe she's right.

Anyway, there was Brenda Tolson, grinning at us. She had the kind of blond hair that's a sort of mixture of light and dark, and blue eyes. She was wearing a T-shirt that said SAVE A SKATER—DRAIN YOUR POOL.

"Thanks, guys," she said, still grinning at us.

She had a chipped tooth right in front, which I thought was kind of cute, and I wondered if she had chipped it in a skateboard accident.

"It was nothing," the Big T said, giving her what he probably thought was an irresistible smile. "We're just glad we were able to help."

He's pretty big already, as I've said, and as he talked to Brenda, his chest swelled out even more than usual. It was a pretty disgusting performance.

He probably thought he looked sharp, but he actually looked like a guy who'd been running through a lot of mud. There were big spots of mud all over his jeans and his Metallica shirt. There was even a little mud in his hair, which would have bothered him a lot if he'd known about it.

"Where did those alligators come from?" Brenda asked.

"We found them in the storm drain," the

Big T said. Even though he said "we," it somehow sounded as if he were saying "I."

By this time the other skate rats had come down from the top of the drain. They gathered around us, and they were all talking at once.

"Wow, those dudes were *gnarly!*" one of them said. It was a guy named Larry Herman. "They must've been six feet long!"

Well, they weren't anywhere near that long, of course, and I tried to set him straight, but he wouldn't listen to me. He kept talking over and over about how big they were and how lucky Brenda was that she hadn't been eaten alive by the giant alligators.

The Big T took over then and more or less implied that Brenda had been saved by his efforts alone and that if it hadn't been for him, the alligators would have eaten not only her but about half the population of Midgeville and the surrounding countryside by now.

That didn't bother me, though. It's just the way the Big T is, and he could take credit for saving anyone he wanted to as far as I was concerned.

What I wanted to know was what had happened to Mike and the alligators.

I started looking around, and I saw Mike about half a block away. He was walking toward us, down the storm drain, not looking too happy, and the alligators were nowhere in sight.

I moved out of the group and went to meet him.

"What happened?" I asked.

He frowned. "They got away," he said.

"Got away?" I looked at the tall, slick sides of the storm drain. "How could they do that?"

"I'll show you," Mike said. "Come on."

As usual, I didn't say anything. I just followed along as he turned and went back in the direction he'd come from.

As we walked, I looked up at either side of the storm drain.

On our left was the street. It was separated from the drain by a sidewalk and a steel mesh fence about five feet high. I thought that it was pretty certain the alligators hadn't been able to escape that way.

On our right, though, there was nothing but

an open field that was choked with tall grass and weeds. I knew that across the field there were houses, but they were cut off from the field by a high wooden fence that I couldn't see from where we were.

Mike saw where I was looking. "They're in the field, all right," he said.

"How did they get there?"

Mike raised his right hand. "That way."

He was pointing at a secondary drain that came right out of the field. In a big rain it would carry the heavy runoff from the residential section and the field behind it. The secondary drain didn't go quite to the bottom of the main culvert where we were, but it was easy to see how the alligators might have climbed up in it and gone off into the field.

"I didn't think it would be a good idea for me to follow them up there," Mike said, more subdued than he usually was. "They could be hiding anywhere in that tall grass."

Knowing him, I was a little surprised that he hadn't just charged right on into the field, armed with nothing except my flashlight, but I was glad he hadn't.

"I think it's time to call the Animal Control officer," I said.

Mike nodded. "I think you're right. You don't think the alligators can get through the fence to where the houses are, do you?"

I thought about the high wooden fence. It was about as solid as a fence could be.

"No," I said. "No way."

"Good," he said.

By that time we had gotten back to where the Big T was still talking to the skate rats.

"It's too bad those gators were so small," he said, flexing his biceps. "Not that the two of them together weren't plenty tough, but they were nothing that couldn't be handled by somebody who knows how."

We managed to get him away from there before he said anything too outrageous. The skate rats left, too. It wasn't the alligators so much as that they didn't want to be there when the Animal Control officer came. The local authorities took a pretty dim view of skateboarding in the storm drain.

"I never realized before how cute Brenda Tolson was," the Big T said as we climbed out of the storm drain.

I didn't say anything. I wasn't as interested in girls as the Big T was, but I have to admit that I was still thinking about that chipped tooth.

The Big T looked around when we got to the top. "What happened to the alligators?" he asked, as if he had just noticed they were gone.

"They're here in the field somewhere," Mike said.

"What? Loose in here with us? Let's get out of here!"

The Big T could move really fast for a guy his size, which is probably why he was such a good football player. He was out of the field and halfway down the side street almost before we knew what was happening.

"Pretty swift moves," Mike said.

"Not bad," I agreed.

By the time we got back to my house, the Big T was breathing normally again. "I could use some more of that grape juice," he said.

We might have gotten some, but Laurie was

waiting for us at the door. "All right," she said. "Where have you been?"

"I hear there's a stage leaving in ten minutes," Mike told her. "Be under it."

She didn't answer him. Instead she said, "I showed Mom that wallet. She said it looked like it had been down in that drain for twenty years. She said you'd better get out of that slimy place and get back here."

"Don't mind my sister," I said to Mike and the Big T. "She just has a dictator complex."

"Right," Mike said. "Where's the phone?"

I showed him. The phone book was under it, and he started looking for the Animal Control officer's number.

Naturally that's when my mother walked in.

"They won't tell me where they've been," Laurie said. "Look at their clothes. I think they've been down in that drain all this time."

"No, we haven't," I said. "We've been chasing alligators."

I hadn't meant to say it right out like that. When you're talking to your mother, or at least to *my* mother, it's usually better to sort of sneak up on the subject when you're going to admit that you've been doing something a little unusual, like chasing alligators. You can start off by talking about how nice the weather is or how nice she looks in her new dress, and work up to the alligators gradually.

But sometimes Laurie gets on my nerves, and I blurt things out. I just can't help it. That's what happened this time.

My mother's reaction was just about what you'd expect.

"Alligators!" she said. Her voice started off high on the "alli" part and then got low when she came to the "gators." "Robert Randall Ross, have you really been chasing alligators?"

"We haven't been chasing them," the Big T said. "We found them in the storm drain, and we thought it was our duty to get them out of there before they invaded the town."

"I think I need to sit down," my mother said. "Why don't we go in the kitchen."

She went and we followed her. She always likes to sit in the kitchen when she's upset.

She sat at the table. "Now let me get this straight," she said. "You've been trying to prevent an alligator invasion of Midgeville, is that right?"

The Big T didn't sound quite as confident as he had when he was talking to Brenda Tolson, but he plunged ahead.

"That's right. There were two of them. Just little ones. We found them in the storm drain."

"And where are they now?" my mother said.

"Uh," the Big T said. Then he didn't say anything else.

"Well?" my mother said. "Where are they now?"

She looked at the Big T first, but he looked down at the floor as if there were something really interesting there. Then she looked at me, and I tried to see what it was the Big T was looking at.

"Yeah," Laurie said. "Where are they now?"

They were both looking at me by then, so I said, "Well, to be honest about it, I think they've invaded Midgeville."

Chapter 8

Calling Mrs. Carver

I thought my mother might faint when I told her that the alligators were on the loose in Midgeville, but she didn't.

It could have been sort of educational if she had, since I don't think I've ever really seen anyone faint. Instead, what she did was put her arm down on the table and then put her head down on her arm and just lie there sighing for a minute or so.

After she was through sighing, she said, "Tell me it isn't true," very softly.

The Big T cracked then. Seeing my mother like that was just too much for him, and I was surprised that he had lasted as long as he had. He probably would have confessed to almost anything just then, like having caused the sinking of the *Titanic* or the extinction of the dinosaurs, if anyone had asked him.

"It's true," he said, all the color draining out of his face. "They've invaded the town, and it's all my fault. I knew we shouldn't have chased them out of the storm drain, and now they're loose in Midgeville and they'll probably do something terrible, like eat someone's pet cat, and we'll have to go to jail for the rest of our lives."

He stopped then, a thoughtful look on his face, as if he might be wondering how we'd all look in white cotton prison suits with our numbers stenciled on the backs.

"It would serve you right if you went to prison," Laurie said. "If those alligators eat my cat, I'll—"

"You don't have a cat," I said, interrupting her, but she wasn't going to let an unimportant detail like the lack of a cat slow her down.

"Well, if I *did* have a cat," she said, "those alligators might eat it, and if they did, you should be sent to prison. It would serve you right."

"No, it wouldn't," Mike said, coming into the kitchen just then. "You don't put heroes in prison. You give them a parade."

"We're going to have a parade?" the Big T asked. He perked right up, and the color came back to his cheeks.

"No parade," Mike said. "But we don't have to worry about the alligators anymore. I called the Animal Control officer."

My mother looked up. "That was a good idea," she said. "Is she going to take care of everything?"

"Well," Mike said, "there's just one little problem."

"I bet she didn't believe you," Laurie said. "I bet she still remembers those goats."

"What goats?" my mother asked. She hadn't heard that story.

"On the baseball field," Laurie said. "One of them butted Coach Emerson."

My mother was looking pretty confused now. "What do goats have to do with any of this?" she asked.

"Not a thing," Mike said. "Not a single thing. It's just that Mrs. Carver wants to talk to an adult. Would you mind?"

My mother ran her hand through her hair. "Who is Mrs. Carver?"

"She's the Animal Control officer," Mike said. "It's not that she doesn't trust me. She'd just like to talk to an adult to confirm what I told her."

"And what did you tell her?"

"About the alligators."

"Oh," my mother said. "All right. I'll talk to her."

She left the kitchen, and the Big T said, "How about some of that grape juice?"

When my mother came back, we were all sitting at the table, drinking grape juice. Laurie had asked the Big T to tell her about the alligators, and he was obliging. He couldn't resist an audience, even if it was only Laurie.

He had just gotten to the part of his story where he single-handedly snatched Brenda Tolson from the horrible gaping jaws of death when my mother entered the room.

67

She didn't look quite as happy as she should have under the circumstances, what with the Animal Control officer taking over and everything. What could be worrying her now?

"What's the matter?" I asked. "Didn't Mrs. Carver believe you?"

"She believed me," my mother said. "At least I *think* she believed me."

"Why shouldn't she believe you?" I asked.

"She wanted to know if my name was Chilton and if I was Mike's mother. She said something about a bunch of flop-eared goats." She looked at Laurie. "Didn't you say something about goats?"

"Never mind the goats," I said before Laurie could open her big mouth. "What about the alligators?"

"She asked me if I'd actually seen the alligators."

"What did you tell her?"

"I told her no, that I hadn't seen them myself, but that my son and his friends had."

I didn't like the way this was going. "But she *is* going to do something about them, isn't she?"

"I think so. I told her that they were dangerous, even if they were small ones. She said that
she would see what she could do."

"Great," I said.

Even Mike looked relieved. We wouldn't
have to worry about the alligators ravaging the
town. The professionals were taking over.

"Is there any of that grape juice left?" my
mother said. "I could use a drink."

I got the grape juice out of the refrigerator,
and Laurie got her a glass.

After the Big T and Mike went home, I spent
most of the afternoon trying to read *Citizen of
the Galaxy*, which is a science-fiction book by
Robert A. Heinlein. I didn't get very far into it,
though. It was an exciting book, but it's hard
to keep your mind on the adventures of some
kid in outer space when you've just had your
own real-life adventure with a pair of alligators.
Where had they come from anyway? And
where had they gone?

Mike called about five o'clock and asked if I
wanted to go to the miniature golf course with
him and the Big T that night. There was more

than just golf there. They had an archery range and some batting cages, too.

"Sounds good to me," I said. "What about the alligators?"

"I guess Mrs. Carver caught them. I haven't heard anything, though." He didn't sound worried. "See you at seven o'clock."

The doorbell rang at seven exactly, and I answered the door. Mike and the Big T were standing there.

My father was sitting in his recliner, reading the newspaper. "Be home by nine," he said. "And don't get into any trouble."

I laughed. My father is a great kidder. Me? Get into trouble?

Just as I was about to shut the door, Laurie and my mother came into the room.

"Would it be all right if Laurie went along?" my mother asked. "You know how much she enjoys playing miniature golf."

The Big T put his hands to his neck and made a noise like he was strangling—*uuuu-uhhhhkkkkkk*—but so low that they couldn't hear him in the house.

Mike didn't say anything. He just looked at me.

There wasn't really anything I could do, though. She *was* my sister, after all, and she did like to play miniature golf.

"All right," I said.

The strangling noise the Big T was making got louder, but no one seemed to notice it.

"Let's go," Laurie said.

Mike gave me another long look, and we went.

One of the nice things about daylight saving time is that it doesn't get dark in the summers until nearly nine o'clock, so my parents don't mind if we walk to the miniature golf course. It's only about six blocks from our house.

As a matter of fact, it's on the very same street that runs right alongside the storm drain, but I wasn't really thinking about that as we walked along.

I was thinking about how much I like the late afternoons in the summertime. It's hot for most of the day, but by seven o'clock the sun is getting lower in the sky, and if there's a breeze, which there usually is, the day begins to get a lot cooler.

As we got closer to the field, though, I thought about the alligators and wondered where they might be. I hoped Mrs. Carver had caught them, but no one had called to let us know that.

Midgeville isn't a very big town, and it doesn't have a mall or a lot of movie theaters or skyscrapers or manufacturing plants or even a lot of traffic. No big-time rock stars ever drop in for a concert, and there's no major league football or baseball team or anything like that. Still, it seems to me like a pretty good place to live, especially on a late afternoon in the summertime.

Except when there are alligators on the loose.

When we passed by the field, Mike, the Big T, and I all stopped and looked through the wire mesh fence.

"What are we stopping for?" Laurie said. "I want to play miniature golf."

"We're looking for alligators," Mike said. "If you want to look a little closer, we'll pitch you over the fence."

"Ha ha," Laurie said. "I'm close enough right here, thank you very much. Anyway, I thought the Animal Control officer took care of the alligators."

That was what I thought, too, but I couldn't help looking.

Nothing moved in the field except for the tall grass that was waving slightly in the breeze. It changed color from brown to gold as the wind moved it from side to side.

There was no sign of any alligators.

"Well," the Big T said, "I guess that's that."

"I guess so," Mike said. "But it was fun while it lasted."

I started to say that alligators weren't any fun at all, when I suddenly realized that I had sort of enjoyed myself that afternoon.

But I didn't say that, either, because there's no telling what Laurie would have told our parents if I had.

Laurie grabbed my shirt and tugged. "Let's go," she said. "I want to play golf."

"All right," I said, letting go of the fence. "But we're going to the batting cages first."

"I don't like the batting cages," Laurie said. "I want to play golf."

"We will," I said. "But batting first, while the light's still good. Right, guys?"

"Right," the Big T and Mike said together.

"Three against one," I said. "Democracy in action."

"Ha ha ha," Laurie said.

Chapter 9

Funtime

Arnold's Golf and Funtime Recreation Park is never very crowded, but there are always a few people there playing golf or hitting baseballs in the cages or shooting at the targets on the archery range.

There was a while there, just after we'd seen an old movie about Robin Hood on cable, that we spent quite a bit of time trying to improve our skills with the bow and arrow, but it turned out that we were no threat to the Prince of Thieves and the Merry Men of Sherwood Forest when it came to hitting the targets.

Not even Mike Gonzo could get the bull's-

75

eye more than once in every twenty or thirty tries, and as for me and the Big T, well, if we'd kept practicing for a few years, we might have managed to put an arrow at least somewhere in the near vicinity of the target. But I wouldn't have counted on it, not unless they made the targets a little bigger.

We weren't really much better in the batting cages, to tell the truth, but there's something really satisfying in hitting a little white ball with a wooden bat, even if you don't manage to do it very often.

Wooden bats. One of the best things about Arnold's Golf and Funtime Recreation Park was that there weren't any of those aluminum bats around at all, and we were glad of it. There's something about the sound of a wooden bat hitting a ball that we really like, and a *clank* is just no substitute.

Besides the wooden bats, another thing we like about Arnold's is the music. We could hear it coming over the loudspeaker even before we got to the park. It's never exactly the same thing, but it's never anything less than twenty years old, either.

This evening it was Dion and the Belmonts, one of Arnold's favorite groups. The song we could hear as we approached was something about a teenager in love.

Arnold himself greeted us at the entrance. He's a big man who looks nearly twice the size of the Big T, and he has a black beard and mustache and long black hair that he wears in a ponytail. He usually dresses like a lumberjack when the weather is cool, but this evening he had on a Hawaiian shirt with red and yellow and green flowers all over it and a pair of red Bermuda shorts. He was wearing sunglasses, and he had a lei of paper flowers around his neck. He was also wearing a blue Houston Oilers cap, which looked a little strange with the rest of his outfit, but that wasn't the kind of thing that bothered Arnold.

"Hey, kids, glad to see ya," he said when we walked up. He moved behind a wooden stand that served as his ticket booth. "What can I do for ya tonight?"

"Three tickets for the batting cage," Mike said.

"Four," Laurie said.

I looked at her, but I didn't say anything. It was her allowance.

We flipped a coin, and the Big T got to hit first. He'd like to play on the Midgeville Middle School Musk Oxen baseball team, but he refuses to wear his glasses on the diamond, so Coach Emerson won't let him try out.

He took off his glasses, put them in his shirt pocket, and stepped into the cage. On the first pitch, he swung and missed.

"I'll hit one when it's my turn," Laurie said. "You just wait."

Well, maybe she would have, but we didn't find out, because that's when the alligators invaded Arnold's.

We found out later that Mrs. Carver, the Animal Control officer, hadn't neglected her job, though we thought at first she might have. She had looked for the alligators all right. She just hadn't found them.

The field they scrambled into that morning was pretty big, after all, and it was full of thick clumps of weeds and even a few old tree trunks. Plenty of good places to hide out if you were an alligator.

And besides, Mrs. Carver wasn't one hundred percent convinced that there really were any alligators there. She had talked to my mother, of course, but she didn't have any witnesses except for Mike and me and the Big T, and she still remembered all those goats, not that we had anything to do with that.

Maybe she didn't look as hard as she could have, but I didn't really blame her. Who would really believe there were alligators roaming loose around Midgeville?

Until that evening at Arnold's, that is.

After that, there were plenty of believers, all right, most of whom had been playing miniature golf at Arnold's when the alligators arrived.

No one ever figured out what had attracted them to the miniature golf course. Some people thought it was the lights, which were already on, since it was getting dusky dark. Others thought the alligators were after the bugs that flew around the lights.

I never agreed with that last idea. I don't

think alligators like to eat bugs. Besides, there weren't all that many bugs to eat, thanks to a couple of electric bug zappers that Arnold had located in strategic places.

Arnold himself thought it was the music that brought the alligators.

"I bet even gators like Dion and the Belmonts," he told the reporters. " 'I Wonder Why' was playing when those little snappers came up on the course, and it's a great song. I bet they wanted to dance. I felt a little bit like dancing, myself."

He went into a kind of dance step then, sort of hopping from one foot to another and spinning around. Someone took a picture of him, and it was in the paper that week.

Maybe it *was* the music that the alligators liked, but whatever it was, they came cruising up onto the eighteenth green just as Jane Ann Walker was lining up the crucial putt that would have allowed her to beat her husband, Leo, at miniature golf for the first time in five years.

Mr. Walker was standing over to the side, telling himself that golf was just a silly game and that it didn't really mean anything if his wife finally beat him after five years.

His wife was beginning her backswing, thoughts of victory filling her head.

"I Wonder Why" was playing on the loudspeakers.

And that's when the alligators showed up.

Arnold's was separated from the field by a chain-link fence, but there was a place in the back where someone's pet dog had dug a hole under the fence.

Arnold knew about the hole, but he hadn't gotten around to filling it in yet. He'd never thought much about the possibility of alligators infiltrating the golf course.

But there they were.

Mrs. Walker saw them first, just as she was about to complete her backswing. She never did complete it. She stood there for a second, frozen, with her club suspended in midair. The alligators were about twenty feet away, close enough for Mrs. Walker to bean one with the ball, if she was that good of a shot.

But instead she screamed, which was the

first time we knew anything strange was going on.

It was a very loud scream, like the ones you hear in the movies sometimes. I can't really describe it, except to say that it made me want to put my hands over my ears, and it even drowned out Dion and the Belmonts.

It didn't bother the alligators a bit. They just kept on coming, swinging their heads from side to side as if they were looking for something.

Maybe they were. It's hard to tell with alligators.

Mrs. Walker was still holding her putter, but she didn't think to use it as a weapon. She just dropped it and started running.

By that time we had left the batting cages, so we saw what happened next. It was kind of sad and funny at the same time.

Mrs. Walker was running as fast as she could from one green to the next. She got across the Dinosaur Valley all right, except for tripping on the baby Stegosaurus, and she scooted around the Laughing Man without missing a step.

But when she turned to look behind her, she

stepped into the moat of the Magic Castle and ran right smack into the castle wall.

The Magic Castle was a lot flimsier than you'd think, and it sort of leaned over away from Mrs. Walker. She lay there on the angle of the wall for a second, and then she slid down the side and into the moat.

Her husband was not far behind her. First he'd taken a couple of swings at the alligators with his club, but he didn't come close to hitting them. He'd thrown the putter down by his wife's club and started after her.

He was pulling her out of the moat when we got there from the batting cages. There was water dripping off her shirt, and her Nike crosstrainers squished when she ran, but that wasn't bothering her at all. She was actually pretty spry for a person her age.

By then there were several other people milling around and trying to figure out what was going on.

"Alligators!" Mr. Walker said as he and his wife ran past them. "We've been attacked by alligators from the sewers!"

Now, I don't want to say anything bad about

Mr. Walker, but it's easy to see how rumors can get started and things can get exaggerated in the heat of the moment.

Technically speaking, those alligators hadn't even come from the storm drain, which is where they had been that morning, much less from the sewers.

They'd come from the field in back of the park. But that wasn't what Mr. Walker said. Maybe he'd seen too many bad movies, but what he said was, "Alligators from the sewers!"

Well, you can imagine what happened when he yelled that out.

People started screaming, and everyone began running toward the entrance to the park.

When the stampede was all over, one of the wings had been broken off the Windmill, Three-Hole Mountain had a couple of extra holes in it, the Volcano looked more like a pancake, and the Laughing Man's moving jaw had been kicked over into Drawbridge River. We could still hear the Laughing Man's maniacal giggles, though, even above the music that was still coming out of the loudspeakers.

Of course, I said "everyone" started running for the entrance, but you've probably already figured out that I didn't really mean that *everybody* did that.

Naturally, Mike Gonzo didn't start running. He stood there, looking back toward where Mr. and Mrs. Walker had come from.

I wish I could explain how he looked just then. There was a big smile on his face, and his eyes were sparkling. He looked about as happy as I'd ever seen him.

"Well," he said, "it looks like Mrs. Carver didn't find the alligators after all."

"Right," the Big T said. "But that's not our fault. We aren't responsible for those things. Let's get out of here."

"We can't do that," Mike said. "Can we, Bob?"

He was looking right at me, his red hair bristling. "Can we?" he said again.

"Of course not," I said.

So instead of heading for the gate like people of normal intelligence, I followed Mike in the other direction.

85

I glanced back, and the Big T was right behind me. Laurie was beside him.

"You'd better leave," I told her.

"No way," she said. "Why should you have all the fun?" Then she frowned. "I'll tell you one thing, though. Those alligators better not have eaten anybody's cat."

I thought I heard the Big T groan, but I wasn't sure. Dion was singing something about being a lonely teenager, and it could have been him instead.

Chapter 10

Alligators in the Moat

It turned out that we weren't the only ones brave enough, or maybe I should say *crazy* enough, to face the alligators. Before we had gone very far, Arnold joined us. It was his golf course, after all, and he must have thought he ought to protect it.

He was carrying a baseball bat that he had probably picked up at the batting cages, and I started to worry a little bit about the safety of the alligators.

I mean, sure, they were scary-looking, and they had sharp teeth, but they hadn't actually hurt anyone yet as far as we knew. They hadn't even eaten any cats. I was glad that Arnold hadn't thought to pick up a bow and arrows. Or maybe he had. Maybe he just wasn't a better shot than the rest of us.

"You kids better get back," Arnold said when we saw the alligators. They were basking in the moat of the Magic Castle, where Mrs. Walker had fallen. "I called 911. The cops'll be here any minute. Until they come, I'll take care of those gators."

He waggled the bat around some, a little like the Big T did before he took a swing at a baseball.

"I don't think you ought to hurt them," Mike said. "I think they might be on the endangered species list."

"The what?" Arnold said.

"Endangered species list," Mike said. "You know. That's a list of all the animals you can't kill because they're in danger of becoming extinct."

"I know two of them that are in danger of becoming extinct, that's for sure," Arnold said, waving the bat around. "Look at my golf course. Those monsters have ruined it."

He started to step into the moat. The alligators were swimming around, their tails waving back and forth in the shallow water. They looked at us as if they were trying to figure out what was going on.

The tops of their heads were out of the water, and every now and then, when their eyes caught the light just right, they glowed red just the way they had that morning in the storm drain.

"They didn't do anything to your golf course," Mike said. "The people who ran away are the ones who did the damage."

Arnold stopped and thought about that. Then he stuck the barrel of the bat down on the green artificial grass and rested the palm of his hand on the knob.

"You're right," he said finally. "I just lost my temper there for a minute. The gators aren't at fault for what happened. They're just a couple of dumb animals."

"Right," Mike said. "So there's no reason to hurt them."

"Right," Arnold said. "I guess we should just

wait for the cops to get here. They can take care of things."

"I'm not so sure about that," Mike said.

"Why not?"

"Well, the police have guns, don't they?" Mike said. "You never know. An innocent alligator could get hurt."

The Big T started to say something else, I think, because his mouth opened and closed a couple of times. He never got a word out, though.

Mike and Arnold were still trying to figure out what to do about the alligators. I may not have mentioned that one of the problems with Mike is that while he's very enthusiastic about doing things, he doesn't always have a clear-cut plan. He just sort of plunges in and then lets things take their course.

In this case, he was all for trying to catch the alligators before the police got there, but he had no idea how to go about doing it.

Neither did I, though I'm not sure Mike wouldn't have tried one of my plans if I had one. In fact, he probably would have, but by then it didn't really matter. While all the talking was going on, the alligators had gotten tired of watching us and decided to move on. They probably weren't quite as dumb as we thought.

They hooked their front feet over the edge of the moat and climbed right out. Then they started walking away in that funny way they had, as if they were just as much at home on artificial grass as they had been in the storm drain.

We stood there watching them waddle for a few seconds, mainly because no one could quite figure out what to do.

Then we realized where they were going.

"They're headed right for the entrance," Mike said. "We can't let them get there."

He was right about that. All the people who had been on the golf course had fled the alligators, but they hadn't gone far. They were all gathered right outside the front gate, and we could see them standing there, looking at us and wondering what we were up to.

And that wasn't all.

Right across the street from Arnold's was Cooper's Supermarket, the biggest grocery store in Midgeville, open twenty-four hours a day. If the alligators were to get out of Arnold's and across the street . . . well, it just didn't bear thinking about.

They had already wreaked considerable havoc with the relatively wide-open golf course. There was no telling what they could do if they were to get into Cooper's.

But of course we weren't going to let that happen. We were going to stop them.

How we were going to stop them, we didn't know. But we were sure that we were going to do it, one way or another.

And if we didn't, then the police would.

Chapter 11

Alligator vs. Bat

I didn't have time to worry about anything for long, though, because Mike said, "Well, what are we waiting for? Come on!"

Now, here's the part that I want to be careful to get right. I know you may have read in the papers about how one of the "sewer monsters" bit a baseball bat in two, but that's not what happened at all.

What happened was this: Arnold took off in a shuffling run and got ahead of us. It was kind of funny to watch him running. He was as big as a bear, and in that Hawaiian shirt, he looked like an explosion in a flower garden.

The alligators were making straight for Drawbridge River, which was about a foot deep, the same as the moat.

The drawbridge was still going slowly up and down. The idea was that you had to time your swing just right so that the ball would get to the bridge when it was down. Otherwise, the ball would wind up in the water and you had to take a two-stroke penalty.

The alligators weren't interested in the bridge, of course. They were interested in the water.

Arnold shuffled along and overtook the alligators. He stood in front of the bridge as if he were protecting it from an invasion.

I don't think the alligators would even have noticed him if he hadn't poked the baseball bat in their faces. (It was the Frank Thomas autograph model, in case you're interested.)

"Don't you hit those alligators!" Laurie yelled.

"I'm not gonna hit 'em," Arnold said, wiggling the bat around. "I'm just gonna keep 'em where they are."

That's what *he* thought.

I don't know what the alligators thought the baseball bat was. They stood very still for a few seconds, just watching it waving around there in front of their noses. Then their heads started moving in tiny circles as they followed its motion.

What came next happened so fast that I'm still not sure whether I saw it or whether I just *think* I saw it. Over short distances alligators can move really *fast*.

Anyway, for one second Arnold was standing there with the bat in his hands, and the next second the bat was out of his hands and in the alligator's mouth.

The alligator waved the bat around for a second or two and then opened its mouth and let the bat clatter to the ground.

"I never felt anything like it," Arnold told the reporters later. "It jerked that bat out of my hands like I was a ninety-eight-pound weakling. I had a good hold on it, too."

Well, that just goes to show that alligators are not just fast. They're also strong.

I saw the bat later, though. It wasn't bitten in two, no matter what you might have read in the papers. It was still all in one piece, though I have to admit that it was pretty chewed and mangled. It looked something like a toothpick might look if you bit down on it and worked it around between your molars for a while.

I hate to think what those teeth could do to a person's arm or leg if they could do that to a piece of solid wood. I was sure it wouldn't be a pretty sight.

Arnold must have been thinking the same thing, because when the alligator dropped the bat, Arnold retreated across the drawbridge and headed for the exit.

"Clear the way!" he yelled. "Here they come!"

He was right. The alligators seemed to have forgotten about the river. I don't think they were chasing Arnold. I think they were just exploring the area.

It must have seemed to Arnold and to the people watching that the alligators were chasing him, though.

The alligators got up on the drawbridge while it was down, and when it started up, they slid down to the other side and followed Arnold toward the gate. They'd have had plenty of room to get out if they needed it, since everyone who had been standing there immediately ran across the street and huddled in the parking lot of Cooper's Supermarket.

"So what are we going to do now?" the Big T asked.

"I don't know," Mike said, and I had to stop and stare at him. I don't think I'd ever heard him say that before.

"I think we should wait for the police," the Big T said.

He wasn't any more eager to grapple with the alligators with his bare hands than Arnold had been, no matter what he'd said to the skate rats that morning.

"I think he's right," Laurie said. "The alligators are already at the gate."

"All right," Mike said, and I could tell he was disappointed. We had missed our chance to be heroes again.

We didn't really have any choice, though. Over the sounds of the golfers, we could hear the sirens of police cars in the distance.

Midgeville's finest were on their way to the rescue.

Chapter 12

The Parking Lot Mess

I want everyone to understand that I'm not blaming what happened next on the police.

It wasn't really their fault, I guess, though I've often wondered why it is that the police never seem to be able to sneak up on anyone.

There's probably a logical purpose for all the flashing lights and squealing brakes and screaming sirens, but I've never figured out just what the reason is, and it certainly had an interesting effect on the alligators that evening at Arnold's.

Generally speaking, alligators don't like to move very fast. In fact, they don't really like to move at all unless there's a pretty good reason.

That morning they'd moved because someone was after them, though I'm still not sure
why they decided to explore the golf course
that evening. But whether it was the music or
the lights or the water, you can bet that they
had a reason.

Even at that, they weren't exactly racing
around that night, just sort of strolling casually
along and reacting to the things around them.

But just about the time they got to the front
gate of Arnold's Golf and Funtime Recreation
Park, the first of the police cars arrived.

It was followed closely by an orange-and-
white EMS vehicle, an ambulance that was
even louder than the police car. I didn't know
why the EMS was there. It may have been that
Arnold was pretty excited when he called 911
and whoever answered decided not to take
any chances.

Right behind the ambulance there were three
or four more black-and-white police cars, red
and blue lights revolving, horns honking, tires
screaming, engines racing.

It was enough to scare anyone, much less a

couple of alligators, who'd probably never seen a police car before, much less an ambulance.

So the alligators stopped meandering and showed everyone that they could really move when they wanted to.

They started running about as fast as anything can run, right across the street and into the parking lot of Cooper's Supermarket.

I think I mentioned that everyone from Arnold's had already crossed the street to where they thought they could watch in safety. They had been joined there by a number of curious shoppers who must have wanted to find out what was going on. I'd say there must have been thirty or forty people standing there in the parking lot, looking across the street.

They didn't stand there long, though, not after the alligators made a beeline for the parking lot.

Grocery bags flew through the air, and cans clattered to the pavement. Bottles shattered, sloshing mustard and ketchup and peanut butter and apple juice all around.

Shopping carts rolled down the slight incline toward the supermarket, bumping into the sides of cars and scraping off the paint as people shoved the carts out of their way.

Car doors slammed as people climbed inside to hide from the charging alligators.

Some people didn't even bother to get into the cars. They just climbed up on the hoods and roofs and stood watching as the alligators rambled on.

We could hear the sounds of metal denting in as people jumped up and down on the car roofs and yelled for help.

You might think that the alligators would have been interested in tasting the mustard, or maybe the peanut butter, but they weren't. They didn't even slow down.

They headed right for the supermarket.

You know how a place like that looks in the early evening, just as the sun is going down. There are fluorescent lights inside, and even a few on the outside, and there's a big neon sign over the entrance that's probably red and blue or some such color. Everything is bright and cheerful and inviting.

So maybe it *was* the lights that the alligators liked. Anyway, for whatever reason, they didn't slow down much in the parking lot, not even when someone standing on top of one of the cars heaved a loaf of bread or a can of green beans at them.

By that time there were police everywhere.

If you've ever been to a circus and seen one of those little cars that seems to hold about fifty clowns, then you know what it looked like that evening at Arnold's.

I counted the police cars later, and there were only five, but there were police pouring out of all of them in what seemed like a never-ending stream.

And of course there were a lot of paramedics who came in the ambulance.

The police were all wearing their black uniforms, and they had all kinds of things dangling from their belts: hard wooden batons (which I thought wouldn't look much better than Arnold's bat if an alligator got hold of one), two-way radios, mace, and pistols.

I thought it must be pretty hard to walk carrying all that equipment, but it didn't seem to bother the police.

They talked excitedly to Arnold first. He

pointed them in the direction of the alligators, and the police took off in hot pursuit.

I was glad that there were so many people in the parking lot because that meant the alligators would be safe from pistol fire. The police wouldn't want to endanger the public.

I guess by this time I was feeling a little sorry for the alligators. I didn't think they were cute, the way some people might; I just thought they were probably lost and confused and looking for a way to get back to wherever it was that they had come from.

The police charged into Cooper's parking lot, and right away three of them slipped down in the mustard and ketchup. Two others tripped over the ones who'd fallen, and there were five police on the pavement at the same time.

When they got up, they looked as if they'd been seriously hurt, with red and yellow stains all over their uniforms. There was probably a little peanut butter in there, too, but it didn't show up as well.

It all looked really scary because of the parking lot lights. I don't know what kind of lights they are, but you've probably seen them in parking lots and other public places like that. They make people's skin look like it has a sickly greenish color, like the zombies in those horror movies your mother won't let you watch on TV.

Kids like to go to Cooper's on Halloween night and stand around making faces and scaring each other.

Well, it wasn't Halloween, but it was pretty weird to see those police with their ketchup-stained uniforms and their ghostly faces. For a few minutes they just stood there, dazed and confused, while their buddies tried to help them clean some of the mess off their uniforms.

The alligators didn't pay any attention to any of that. They just went on into the super-market.

It was easy for them to get inside. Cooper's has those automatic doors that open when you step on a pressure pad in front of them.

A three-foot alligator weighs a lot more than you'd think. When they put their front feet on the pad, the doors opened right up, and the alli-gators marched right on in.

I don't know what the alligators thought when they got inside, but the shoppers were certainly surprised.

The manager of the store told the TV reporters later that it would take at least a full day to get the store cleaned up and to get everything back in its place.

The customers dropped milk cartons and packages of spaghetti, ran into displays of stacked cans and scattered them everywhere, tried to climb the shelves and knocked cans of soup and coffee into the aisles, stood in the open freezers in the meat market until their feet got so cold they couldn't stand there any longer, and climbed over the front of the Courtesy Booth to hide inside.

I would have liked to have seen the damage on TV, along with nearly everyone else in town, but of course it didn't work out that way. I got to see most of it for myself when Mike Gonzo led us past the police officers, intent on following the alligators right into the supermarket.

Chapter 13

To Market, to Market

I don't think the police are going to be able to handle this," Mike said. He was standing in front of the supermarket, looking at the situation in the parking lot. We'd managed to avoid the worst of the spills in the lot. I got a little apricot jelly on one shoe, but that was all.

"And it's bound to be even worse inside the store," Mike predicted.

"I'll bet the police will do just fine," the Big T said. "They're professionals, don't forget. They know how to deal with a crisis."

"They have ketchup on their uniforms," Mike said.

"Yeah, well, that's true, but that doesn't mean we have to go getting mixed up in things," the Big T said.

Just as he said it one of the police, a tall woman with short blond hair that stuck out from under the edges of her cap, left the group and started to make her way down toward the supermarket.

She didn't get very far at all before she stepped in a big glop of something slick, mustard probably, or maybe ketchup, and both feet slid out from under her. She landed hard on her rear end, and three other police went running to help her up.

One of them fell, too.

"You see what I mean?" Mike asked.

We saw.

"Well, then, what are we waiting for?" Mike started for the door.

We followed him, as usual. I started to tell Laurie to go back, but she had such a determined look on her face that I didn't bother. When she looks like that, there's no sense in trying to argue with her.

There were a lot of shopping carts in front

of the entrance. They'd rolled there from all over the parking lot. We shoved them aside and went through the automatic doors.

When we got inside the store, it was very quiet. We could hear music (not Dion and the Belmonts) playing over the speaker system, but that was all.

We stood for a while and listened. Every now and then there would be a scream, followed by a crash, so we thought we would be able to track the alligators pretty easily.

There were a couple of cashiers standing on the counters by their cash registers. They didn't say anything to us as we went by. They were up on their tiptoes, trying to see where the alligators were.

"Be careful," Mike said.

"Why are you whispering?" the Big T said. "Do you think they can hear us?"

"Who knows?" Mike said. "I just don't believe in taking chances."

"Oh. Right," the Big T said. Very quietly.

We went through one of the cashier's lanes, moving aside a shopping cart loaded with groceries and also a small man who was sitting on top of them with his legs dangling over the side of the cart.

"There are alligators back there," the man said. "They came right by here."

"We know," Mike said, slipping into that voice that adults always responded so well to. "We're going to catch them."

"Alligators are very dangerous, you know," the man said.

"We know," Mike said. He sounded a lot calmer than I felt. "But we know how to handle them."

"We do?" the Big T said.

"Remember what you were telling Brenda Tolson?" I said. "You know all about it."

"Who's Brenda Tolson?" Laurie asked.

"Never mind," I said.

We were standing in the row of the supermarket where the sign said we could find BAK- ING GOODS, SUGAR, SPICES. Lying in the aisle were several sacks of sugar broken open, and a woman was clinging to the top shelf to our left.

"There are alligators in here," she said.

"We know," we all said together, walking

down the aisle, the sugar crunching under our feet.

"I think they're over to the right about three rows," Mike said. "That's where the last scream came from."

"Maybe I'd better stay here while you check it out," the Big T said. "I'll make sure they don't double back on you."

"I think we'd better stick together for now," Mike said. "I've got a plan."

"You do?" I said.

"Sure I do. You don't think I'd just come in here after two alligators if I didn't have a plan, do you?"

Well, that's exactly what I had been thinking, since he usually never had a plan, but I didn't think that this was the right time to admit it.

"I guess not," I lied. "What's the plan?"

"Follow me," Mike said.

"That doesn't sound like much of a plan," Laurie said, but she followed him, just like the rest of us.

We went down the aisle to the back of the store where the meat counter was. We followed the meat counter until we came to the aisle where shoppers could find PET FOOD, PET SUP-PLIES, PAPER GOODS.

We still hadn't seen the alligators, but we heard a squeal from two aisles farther on.

"They're still moving around," Mike said. "Good."

He didn't explain why it was good, and we didn't ask him. He started looking at the pet supplies.

"What are you going to do?" the Big T asked. "Get them a rubber bone to chew on? Maybe a cat toy to play with?"

Mike didn't answer. He stepped over several sacks of cat food that were lying in the aisle and kept on walking along until he came to the dog leashes.

There were several kinds. Some of them were made of chain links, some were made of what looked like braided plastic fibers, and some were made of leather.

"I think the leather will work best," Mike said. He took several off the hook and gave one to me and one to the Big T.

"What about me?" Laurie said.

He handed one to her, too.

"We're going to leash them?" the Big T said. For an old alligator handler, he looked a little panicky to me. "We're going to put leashes on alligators? How are we going to do that? I didn't notice that they were wearing collars."

"Yeah," Laurie said. "I didn't, either."

She might be my little sister, but I'll have to admit she was too smart to want to get close to an alligator with just a dog leash in her hand.

"And even if they do have collars, I don't think they're going to just stand there and let us snap a leash on!" the Big T said.

"Let's try to discuss this calmly," Mike said.

"I'm calm!" the Big T shouted. "Who said I wasn't calm?"

"If you're so calm, then why are you yelling?" Laurie asked.

"I'm not yelling!" the Big T yelled. His voice bounced off the hard floor and echoed around the supermarket.

We all looked at him.

"I'm not yelling," he said again, but quieter this time.

"Good," Mike said. "Now what do we know about alligators?"

"They're green and they're knobby and they might eat someone's cat," Laurie said.

"Besides that," Mike said.

We thought about it for a minute.

"Not very much," I said. "They're strong and they're fast, but that's about all."

"Maybe that's all you know," Mike said, "but I went to the library this afternoon and read some books about alligators. I found out some pretty interesting facts."

Now, that was one of the things that always surprised me about Mike, though I don't know why it should. You'd expect someone like him, someone who always liked to *do* things and to be in the middle of the action, to be the kind of person who didn't much like to read books.

But you'd be wrong, just the way I was wrong when I thought that the skateboarders would all be boys. You just can't be sure about things like that.

Mike was interested in doing all kinds of things, all right, but he wasn't interested in just doing them. He was interested in finding out about them and learning about them from books, too.

"What did you find out?" the Big T asked.

"Did you see what happened to Arnold's bat when the alligator bit down on it?" Mike asked.

"I wish you hadn't mentioned that," the Big T said.

"Well, that's an example of how strong an alligator's jaws are," Mike said. "They can put thousands of pounds of pressure on something when they bite down like that."

"Boy, that's a really comforting thought," the Big T said, looking at the leash he was holding. "I'm really glad you shared that with me. So what good is this little skinny piece of leather going to do?"

"That's the interesting part," Mike said. "An alligator's jaws don't work both ways."

"Sure they do," Laurie said. "They can open their mouths really wide. I saw them."

"They can open them, all right," Mike said, "but the muscles that open them aren't very strong. A little kid could hold an alligator's mouth shut with one hand."

"You read that in a book, right?" the Big T said.

"That's right," Mike told him. "A book about alligators."

The Big T wasn't convinced. "What if the book was wrong?"

"It wasn't wrong. There was a picture of a man holding an alligator's mouth shut. He was only using two fingers and his thumb."

"It was probably a *tame* alligator," the Big T said. "I don't think the two in here are going to let us get close enough to hold their mouths shut."

Laurie looked at her fingers. "I'm not sure I even want to try," she said.

"That's what the leashes are for," Mike said.

There was a silver clip on one end of the leash he was holding. He ran that end through the loop on the other end to make a noose and held it up for us to see.

"A lasso," he said. "We slip the noose over the alligator's snout, pull it tight, and we've got him."

The Big T looked at Mike's leash. "It's pretty short," he said. "We're still going to have to get awful close to the alligators to put it on them. How do you know they'll cooperate with us?"

"Well, I don't know that they will," Mike said. "That's the part of the plan I haven't quite figured out yet."

I was afraid of that. He'd had more of a plan than I expected, but it didn't go quite far enough.

"Anyway, we've got to try," he said. "The police are going to be coming in here any minute, and when they come we're going to have to keep out of the way."

"Maybe that's a good idea," the Big T said. "They're the—"

"—professionals," Mike said. "You said that already. But I don't think they know any more about alligators than we do. I'm not even sure they know as *much* about them as we do. Maybe they haven't read the book. So it's up to us."

Something about the way he said it convinced me that he was right, and I could see that he had somehow convinced the Big T and Laurie as well.

"All right," I said. "But what do we do now?"

"I was hoping you might have some idea about that," he said.

"Me?" I said.

They were all looking at me, even Mike.

"Well," I said, "maybe I do have an idea, at that."

And then I told them what it was.

Chapter 14

A Trip Down the Aisle

I was making my way down the aisle that stocked DETERGENTS, CLEANSERS, HOUSEHOLD CLEANING SUPPLIES, but I wasn't walking on the floor.

I was sliding my feet along the third shelf up, trying to keep from knocking off plastic bottles of dishwasher detergent, boxes of laundry soap, cans of household deodorizer, and packages of TideeToidy.

It wasn't easy.

I had to hold on to the top shelf with my hands while I slid my feet along and tried not to lose my balance. I had the leash in my mouth between my teeth, and I was already beginning to wonder how I was going to carry out the rest of my plan.

It hadn't taken long for everyone to see that it wasn't a very good plan, but since no one could come up with a better one, we decided to give it a try.

It was pretty simple.

Mike would start at one end of the aisle where the alligators were, and I would start at the other. We would move along the shelves, high enough up so that the alligators couldn't reach us unless they could climb.

"But what if they *can* climb?" the Big T asked.

"They can't," Mike said. "It didn't mention climbing in the book."

"That doesn't mean they can't do it," Laurie said.

"Did you ever see an alligator in a tree?" Mike asked.

Laurie hadn't, and neither had the Big T or I.

"Then they can't climb," Mike said.

It sounded logical to me, but then I'd never

seen an alligator in a grocery store, either, and there they were.

So maybe Mike was wrong about the climbing. If he was, we were going to be in big trouble.

"Maybe we ought to use the chains instead of the leather," the Big T said. "Those alligators can bite leather right in two."

It was a good thought, but Mike said the chains wouldn't work. "They knot up," he said. "You can't make a good noose with them."

The Big T had to agree, but he still looked as if he would have preferred to use chains. It would have been pretty hard on our teeth if we had, though.

We left The Big T and Laurie to watch for the police and to tell them that everything was under control. They both seemed to think that was a good idea.

"I might be too heavy to climb on those shelves," the Big T said. "I wouldn't want to be responsible for breaking anything."

"Do you think the police will believe us

when we tell them that you have everything under control?" Laurie asked.

That was a good question.

I wish I'd had a good answer for it.

I maneuvered my way past the bleach, knocking off only a one-quart plastic bottle. It hit the floor with a kind of a *ploop*, but the top didn't come off, and it didn't seem to bother the alligators, who were located near the middle of the aisle.

One alligator was looking one way, at me, and one was looking the other way, at Mike.

Or maybe they were thinking about buying a few boxes of laundry detergent to clean up with when they got back to the swamp. It was hard to tell.

As I got closer to the alligators, I noticed that my hands were sweating. They seemed to be slipping a little as I tried to grasp the shelving.

That was just great. I'd probably get right by the alligators, and my hands would slip, and I would fall off the shelf into their wide-open jaws.

I thought about the way the alligator had

chewed Arnold's baseball bat, and my hands started to sweat even more.

I was really good at cheering myself up.

Then I looked at the alligators and saw something that encouraged me a little. Their jaws weren't open.

If the alligators had their mouths open, there would be no way at all to get the loop over them unless I could think of some way to get them closed.

I couldn't think of one, not unless I got them to close their jaws on something like my arm or my leg, and I didn't even want to consider that possibility.

Even with the jaws closed, getting a loop over them wasn't going to be easy. I hadn't had much practice at roping alligators, or at roping anything else for that matter.

I clamped my teeth down on the leash and inched my way along the shelf, hoping for the best.

That was when I heard the bullhorn.

I forgot to mention bullhorns when I was talking about the police. They amplify your voice electronically, and they're another way the police have of making a whole lot of noise when they come into a place. They were making a lot of noise now.

"ATTENTION! ATTENTION! ATTENTION!" the police voice said. It was a little staticky, but I could understand it all right.

I don't know whether the alligators understood, but they looked up alertly. That was just what we needed, something to make them even more watchful than they were already.

"WE WANT EVERYONE TO CLIMB DOWN OFF THE COUNTERS AND SHELVES AND PLEASE LEAVE THE PREMISES!" the voice on the bullhorn continued. "PLEASE WATCH YOUR STEP!"

It was quiet for a minute, and we could hear people knocking off cans of pinto beans and crushed pineapple as they climbed off the shelves.

"PLEASE PROCEED IN AN ORDERLY MANNER TO THE EXIT AT THE FRONT OF THE STORE," the voice said. "UNIFORMED OFFICERS WILL BE WAITING OUTSIDE TO TAKE YOUR STATEMENTS."

I saw the Big T's head pop around the end of the aisle in front of me. Just his head, though.

He wasn't going to risk exposing his entire body to the alligators.

"P-s-s-s-s-t," he hissed. "We've got to leave. The police are here."

I took the leash out of my mouth. It left a leathery taste. "I can hear them," I said.

"IT IS OUR UNDERSTANDING THAT THERE ARE AL-LIGATORS IN THE STORE, AND WE ARE HERE TO DEAL WITH THE PERPETRATORS," the voice said.

"Uh-oh," the Big T said. "What's a *perpetrator?* Does that mean us?"

"PLEASE REMAIN CALM!" the voice said. "PRO-CEED IN AN ORDERLY MANNER!"

We could hear loud voices and the sound of running feet as the people in the store reached the front doors. I thought I heard someone yelling about "monsters from the sewers," and I wondered if Mr. and Mrs. Walker had been hiding in the store.

"DO NOT SHOVE!" the voice said.

There was a loud, crashing, staticky sound as the bullhorn hit the floor and rolled around. We found out later that the police had all been pushed out of the store by the surging crowd of shoppers. It took them ten minutes to sort things out and get back inside.

But the Big T didn't know that at the time.

"P-s-s-s-s-s-t!" he hissed again. "Are you guys coming, or what?"

We were almost to the alligators, and I knew what Mike was going to say.

He said, "No. You go ahead. We'll be through here in a second."

I'll say this for the Big T. He was loyal.

"No," he said. "I'll stay here just in case."

"Me, too," a loud voice said.

"Yah-h-h-h-h-h-h!" the Big T yelled, jumping straight up. He had a pretty good vertical leap for such a big guy.

When he came down, he looked around, and there was Laurie, standing right behind him.

"Don't *do* that!" he said.

Laurie just smiled at him.

"All right," Mike said. He'd reached the alligator he'd planned on roping, and I could see by the look in his eye that he lived for moments like this. "Are you ready, Bob?" he asked.

I wasn't really ready, but what could I say? "Sure," I told him.

"Let's do it," he said.

He held on to the top shelf with one hand, leaned down, and dropped the noose over the alligator's nose as if he'd been practicing it for weeks. Mike was almost graceful as he performed his stunt; and the alligator just sat there like somebody's pet who was ready for its evening walk.

Mike pulled the noose tight and smiled at me. "Nothing to it," he said. "Now it's your turn."

So I took the leash, leaned out, and fell right into the aisle.

Chapter 15

Closing the Jaws of Death

I tried to grab hold of something to keep from falling, but all I did was sweep my arm down the shelf and bring a rain of clear plastic bottles of glass cleaner and blue bricks of TideeToidy down with me.

I tried to cover my head as the cleaning items cascaded down, and when I did, I found myself face to face with the alligator.

It wasn't one of the best moments of my life. In fact, as I stared into the alligator's beady black eyes, I was about as scared as I'd ever been before.

Why did I let Mike Gonzo talk me into these things?

Then I realized that I'd dropped the leash and didn't have any idea where it was, and I got even more scared.

The alligator opened its mouth. I could see all those sharp, white teeth, and I could smell its breath, which was really rotten but which was the least of my worries just then.

"The leash!" Mike said. "Where's the leash?"

I could see his feet by the alligator, but for some reason I couldn't look away from that open mouth.

"I don't know," I said, trying to wiggle backward.

I got about a foot, and the alligator took a step toward me.

I heard Mike kicking aside the plastic bottles as he searched for the leash.

"I can't find it!" he said.

I wiggled backward.

The alligator took another step.

I tried to wiggle backward again and hit the bottom of the shelving.

The alligator smiled and opened wider.

I closed my eyes.

I wish I hadn't, since what happened next must have been quite a sight, and I would have enjoyed seeing it.

As Mike described it to me later, the Big T, a leash between his teeth, came gliding down the aisle as gracefully as an ice skater, which is not unlikely. The Big T is really light on his feet for such a big guy.

He came up behind the alligator, put one hand on its upper jaw and the other on its lower jaw, and closed its mouth.

Then he said, "Take 'ee le'esh."

Mike took the leash from the Big T's mouth and slipped the noose over the alligator's jaws. Mike tightened the noose, the Big T let go, and neither alligator was any longer a threat.

"You know, that alligator could have bitten your fingers off," Mike said.

"I know," the Big T said. "I think I'd better sit down."

He dropped down beside me and let out his breath in a long sigh.

"Thanks," I said.

*   *   *

129

Things moved pretty fast after that.

We made sure the leashes were secure around the alligators' jaws, and then we waited for the police to find us.

It took them a little while, but when they got there, they got there in force. About fifteen heads popped around the end of the aisle.

They looked a little surprised to see four kids along with the alligators, and they were even more surprised when they saw that we seemed to be all right.

One of the police lifted a bullhorn and said, "ALL RIGHT, KIDS, YOU'RE SAFE NOW. MOVE SLOWLY AWAY FROM THE ALLIGATORS, AND WE'LL TAKE CARE OF THEM."

Since he was standing only about fifteen feet away, he didn't really need the bullhorn, but maybe he just loved to use it.

"We've already taken care of them," Mike said. He held up a leash. "They can't hurt anyone if their mouths are tied shut."

The police talked among themselves for a minute, and then one of them started cautiously down the aisle toward us. He had dark red stains on his uniform. Probably ketchup, I decided.

When he got to us, he inspected the leashes. They must have seemed sturdy enough to him because he turned and motioned to the others, and a couple of them came toward us.

"Good job, kids," the policeman said. "We'll take over now."

He reached out his hand for the leashes, and that's when the TV crew arrived.

We don't have a TV station in Midgeville, but a crew from a nearby city had been taping a rodeo not far away. When they heard about the sewer monsters, they naturally came running.

They got some good shots of Mike and the Big T handing over the leashes to the police, and then they got an interview with the Big T.

He couldn't resist telling them about my falling off the shelves and landing on my leash so no one could find it and about how he had to rescue me from certain death in the alligator's jaws.

He told them about how we'd discovered the alligators that morning and how he had saved the skateboarders from toothy doom, with virtually no help at all from his pals.

If world peace had broken out about that time, he would probably have taken credit for that, too, but by then I had stopped listening. I didn't even watch him on the news that night.

We walked home after it was all over. So much had happened, it seemed as if hours had passed, but it wasn't even nine o'clock. We were going to be home on time.

When we were walking along the sidewalk by the storm drain, we talked a little about everything that had happened.

After the TV crew left, the police had called Mrs. Carver, and she had come to the store to get the alligators. She said that she would see that they were returned to one of the local lakes, which is where they had probably come from in the first place.

"Wasn't it great?" Mike said. "We captured the alligators and saved the town, just like I knew we would."

"You didn't know that," Laurie said. "You

thought Mrs. Carver caught them this morning."

She didn't bother Mike, though. "We're going to be on TV," he said. "We're heroes."

Actually, it was the Big T who was going to get most of the credit, but I could see that didn't bother Mike, either. The adventure of the thing was all that mattered to him, not getting his face on TV.

The Big T agreed with Mike. "It was great, all right," he said. "I wonder what we can do for an encore?"

"Who knows?" Mike said.

We walked on toward my house. The moon was coming up now, big and yellow, and the stars were coming out.

"I hope those alligators didn't eat anyone's cat," Laurie said.

The Big T wasn't worried about anything like that. "I wonder how I'll look on TV?" he said. "I hope Brenda Tolson is watching."

"I hope she isn't," I said. "Anyway, next time—"

"Next time?" the Big T said.

"Right!" Mike said. "Next time!" He

133

stopped and looked around. "Who knows what adventures are out there waiting for us? Today, alligators! Tomorrow—who knows!"

"Alligators were bad enough," the Big T said, not really so eager for an encore after all. "If there's anything else, you can count me out."

"We'll see about that," Mike said, and his eyes were shining. "We'll see."

Something else came along, all right, but we didn't see it. That's because it's impossible to see an invisible man.

But I guess that's another story.

About the Author

BILL CRIDER teaches English at Alvin Community College in Alvin, Texas, and insists that neither the town nor the college was named for a singing chipmunk. Besides the books in the Mike Gonzo series, he is the author of *A Vampire Named Fred* and more than thirty mystery, Western, and horror novels for adults. He likes alligators, cats, paperback books, and old baseball cards.

MiKE GONZO

Jump into gear with Mike Gonzo
as he meets spooky monsters
and out of this world aliens...

#1 **MiKE GONZO** and the Sewer Monster
NOW AVAILABLE

#2 **MiKE GONZO** and the Almost Invisible Man
COMING SOON!

#3 **MiKE GONZO** and the UFO Terror
COMING SOON!

By Bill Crider

A MINSTREL® BOOK
Published by Pocket Books

1259-01